The Divine Chronicles

Divine Awakening

A Novella

Awaken your Destiny!

JoAnna Grace

JoAnna Grace

Divine Awakening

Published 2013 by Winged J Press

Cover Design by Once Upon a Time Covers
Formatting by Champagne Formats

ISBN: 978-1-940460-05-5

Other Books by JoAnna Grace

The Divine Chronicles
Divine Awakening: Prequel Novella to Divine Destiny
Divine Destiny
Divine Judgment

The Blake Pride Series
Pride Before The Fall
Break Her Fall

The Roles We Play

DEDICATION

To every woman that has ever fallen on her rear end in front of *that* guy,
and to every guy who loved her anyway.

CHAPTER ONE

A TREMOR WENT up her spine. Her breath became lodged in her chest. She rubbed her sternum, hoping to relieve the mysterious pressure. Avery looked up from the table she was clearing to see two men walk into her café. One she recognized and one she didn't. It was the stranger who captured her attention.

Even in a simple gray shirt he looked ready to take someone's head off. He had to be bordering on six and a half feet and his shoulders were as wide as a barn door. Not an inch of fat to be found. The cotton shirt stretched over every bulge and dip of his muscles. When deep brown eyes met hers, her pulse hiccupped, and she gasped.

The world froze. She couldn't help but stare, which was why she dropped the cup in her hands and sent it crashing to the floor. The mug shattered and coffee splashed everywhere. Idiot! She bent to clean up the mess. Why did she have to do something so clumsy in front of someone so handsome?

"Let me help you." Two large hands scooped up the pieces of the mug.

Avery's eyes shot up and met with the stranger's again. The staggering weight of his presence made her fall over. The minute her body started to shift, the man reached out and grabbed her elbow. A zing of current went up her arm. She would've fallen right on her ass.

"Easy there." When he spoke again, Avery swore that angels began to sing. His lips were delectably full and she watched them move.

You should come with a warning label, Avery thought as she let out a nervous laugh. When he smiled and his cheeks tinted pink, she realized she'd said that out loud. Mortified, she jerked upwards and whopped her head on the table.

"Damn it!" She rubbed the sore spot. The delicious stranger stood and placed the pieces of the broken mug on her tray.

"Let me look at that. You might have a cut." Acting as if he owned the rights, he stepped in close and used his hands to tilt her head to see.

She stopped breathing for a moment. His hands were warm and soft on her skin. She could only imagine how they would feel when he touched a lover. The lustful thought made her suck in air. His scent nearly knocked her back to the floor. It was a combination of spring in the woods, hints of earth and crisp mountain air, and fresh rain on leaves. Notes of exotic spices that begged to be tasted and savored. Dear god, she wanted to roll in his scent until it was embedded into her pores.

"Great cologne," she whispered, because she didn't have much oxygen left.

"Oh." He looked from her head back to her eyes. His brows dipped. "I'm not wearing any. But thank you."

Damn. This man was dangerous with a capital D. Taking a step back, Avery tried like hell to gain her composure. Their whole interaction had only taken a minute.

"I'm fine. Really. Please have a seat and I'll be right with you." She gathered up the dirty and broken dishes and walked into the kitchen.

"Oh. My. God. That man is a walking orgasm inducer," Izzy, her best friend—and best employee—said as Avery closed her eyes for a moment. "I'm all hot and bothered, and he didn't even touch me. You must need a cigarette."

Avery chuckled and shook her head. "He's just a man, Izz. Just a man."

"Well let's pray that he's just a man that wants a feisty blonde woman to have his babies, shall we?" Izzy fluffed her corkscrew blonde hair and adjusted her top so her boobs were pushed up even higher. "C'mon girls, Mama needs a boyfriend."

"Izz. No."

Her friend blanched. "What? Why?"

"Cause I have dibbs." Avery and Izzy were still for a second before they both bolted for the door to the dining room. The minute they exited, they were composed except for the matching grins.

"Can I have the young, blue-eyed one at least?" Izzy whispered and grabbed some menus.

"He's a new officer with Frank and Jerry. Keep that in mind." Both Frank and Jerry had claimed the girls as sisters and had a tendency to scare off any men who made a play at the girls.

"I think Mr. Muscle can take 'em both."

Avery sidled up to the table before Izzy, who winked as she walked on to the next group of customers. "G'morning. What can I get you gentleman?" Avery kept her eyes on the notepad in her hand. If she looked up, her brain might misfire again.

"Your name would be a great start."

Since that was the last damn thing she expected, Avery glanced up at the handsome stranger. Once again, her brain stopped working and she stood there with her mouth hanging open like a moron.

As if he noticed the awkward silence, the blue-eyed guy chuckled. "The bacon and egg platter for me, please. Over easy. No personal information on the side."

Avery tried to smile or laugh or something except stare at the man who left her speechless. Dang, she had to get it together. She had a café to run here. With a slight headshake, she focused on the man ordering.

"Right. Bacon and eggs, over easy." She clarified and then turned to the flirt. "And what would you like to eat, sir?"

As soon as the words left her mouth, she regretted her phrasing. The man's eyes drifted down the length of her body and back up before he quirked a brow and tilted his head. He licked his bottom lip and Avery saw stars dance in her vision. One corner of his mouth pulled back. It didn't take a genius to figure out exactly what he was thinking. Her body went rigid. The apron over her chest was too tight. The heat in his eyes when he grinned was enough to set her insides on fire.

"From the menu," she spit out before he could say something that made her blush more than she already was. "What would you like from the menu?"

"Same as he's having." The two men exchanged a look.

The blue-eyed one shook his head at his friend. Avery had seen him around once before and knew he was new to town and the police station. Since all the officers came to the café, Avery treated them like family. This rookie would be no different, so she didn't give him special treatment.

Using the two menus she lightly hit him on the shoulder. "Behave."

He held his hands up in surrender. "I am! He's the one trying to get all personal." He snickered as Avery walked off then spoke to his friend. "You shouldn't do that to her, man. You're going to make her pass out."

"I don't think so. She's tough."

Avery shouldn't have heard their words, but their voices drifted to her over the crowd. Before she walked through the doors of the kitchen, she glanced back at the men. Blue-eyes stared at something out the window. But her sexy stranger focused on her. When he winked, she couldn't help flashing him a quick smile in return.

It was hard to work knowing he watched. She'd waited on her other customers as normal, but she could feel his eyes track her movements. He was a force of gravity pulling her body in every time she wandered too close. The coffee in his cup had never been an inch lower than the rim.

Thankfully two of her favorite people came in and offered a needed distraction. Frank had been her friend since grade school, when they'd gotten into trouble together over setting frogs loose in the classroom. Since then they'd been inseparable. Frank was her age, but the job had made him older. He was a police officer, same as all the other men in his family. Frank had always been her personal protector. When her parents had been killed in a car accident, Frank had delivered the news. They had history.

With him came Jerry. He'd joined the police force a couple years ago and was Frank's partner. Jerry had one goal in life: to get under Frank's skin. His most common tool of aggravation was flirting with Avery.

"Hey baby girl!" Jerry slapped a wet kiss on Avery's cheek and draped his arm over her shoulder. "You working hard or hardly working?"

Avery glanced over to see if her stranger was watching. He was. His eyes were glued to the scene and he didn't look pleased.

"You know me." Avery slipped out of Jerry's hold. "Try to keep moving 'til I fall over."

Frank gave his usual greeting. "Hey kiddo." He hugged her, then let out a huge yawn.

"Night shift?" Avery guessed as she poured them coffee.

"Yep. And wouldn't you know, there was a party in one of the subdivisions. Got five calls about the noise. Damn kids." Frank huffed and sipped the black coffee.

"Don't act so holy. We used to be those damned kids that partied all the time." Avery gave him an affectionate wink. Frank couldn't deny it. Back in their youth they'd been troublemakers.

"Speaking of parties," Jerry chimed in. "Avery, you have to come out with us tomorrow night. We're going to Marshall's to kick up our heels. I need a date, baby girl." He kept rubbing his neck and rolling his shoulders.

"No dates, you know that. But I'm in. What's with your neck? You're really tense." She rubbed his shoulders until his head fell forward and he sighed.

"Oh, nothing. Just need some sleep. I think I'm going to head out. Thanks for the coffee." Jerry left the café without another word. Poor guy, he must have been exhausted.

Blue-eyes came to the bar to talk to Frank. Avery overheard them agree to meet at Marshall's Bar. But her attention was on the stranger. He motioned her over with two fingers.

"Enjoy your meal?" Avery gathered up his empty plate, but he stilled her hands.

He placed his hand on her hip and she froze; her heart kicked up in her chest.

"Have dinner with me."

Avery narrowed her eyes. Excitement flooded her brain and her southern accent thickened when she spoke. "Are you askin' or tellin'?

Because that's gonna determine my answer."

His lips quirked. "Begging."

Oh hell.

"I—I don't know you."

He squinted and whispered, "Hence the need for a dinner date."

Damn he was sexy with his smartass remarks. He kneaded her hip and she naturally leaned into his hold. Hell, she wanted to crawl into his lap and snuggle her face into his neck.

What on earth is wrong with me? She never reacted to a man in such a way.

"I don't know your name."

"Ryse."

Ryse, like the candy. How fitting. She thought about all the things she wanted to do with that candy. Avery took a deep breath and pulled out her order pad from her apron pocket. She scribbled down her information and ripped the sheet off.

"I close at six on Fridays."

Ryse looked at the name and number. This piece of information was his prized possession. The instant he'd walked in and her gorgeous green eyes met his, he knew this was the woman he was searching for. There was no doubt about it. Those eyes alone could have convinced him. The finest gems didn't compare to their depth and beauty. His hands itched to touch the soft skin of her heart-shaped face or remove the clip that held back a thick mane of luscious brown curls. Her curvy frame was just the right height, not too tall or too short. She would fit perfectly in his arms.

By the gods, she was remarkable! It took every lesson of control he'd ever learned to keep his hands off her. Odd, since he never wanted to touch or be touched by anyone.

Avery had waved shyly when he left. Walking out of that café was the hardest thing he'd ever done. Somewhere in this town was a rogue. And that bastard was after Avery. If Ryse didn't figure out who it was quickly, her life might be in danger.

A couple weeks ago, Bren had come to the area and confirmed something was going on. He could sense the traces of a powerful Olympian aura, but couldn't pinpoint the source. Once Bren had visited the café a couple times, he knew it was Avery. Ryse arrived and felt the same pull.

"See what I mean?" The boy had said when they left the café. "It's like power buried beneath the earth just waiting to erupt."

"Her aura is blocked. It's a good thing. Our presence will cause it to surface. Whoever is watching her knows we're here. We have to be on guard."

Brenden had kept up with Avery's movements via GPS. Three cameras were installed in her home, one in her café and a tracker on her car. They were missing something and her safety took precedence over her privacy.

The Elites, Ryse's personal squad of Olympian soldiers, had set up a base of operations with modern technology. Cutter, his master swordsman, hacked into the local police database and ran facial recognition on everyone who came into the café. Philippe, an Elementalist, kept his eyes on any atmospheric changes caused by a powerful Olympian using their magic. Yankee—well, Yankee was there to eat until there was an actual fight. Then his unparalleled strength and speed would benefit the group. Until then, he watched the video feed of her house.

"Master." Hammon, the senior member of his Elites and their tracker, sat in meditation. His eyes glowed with the use of his abilities. "I sense something. It is not the woman. Something much more powerful is in the area."

Yankee noticed something on the screen at the same time. "Someone is in her house!"

CHAPTER TWO

THEY HAD ARRIVED. He could sense the auras of Thracian soldiers around town. They too were shielding themselves, same as he was. If the gods sent in Thracians, and an especially potent one, the girl must be special after all. He had to make sure.

Sweat beaded on his forehead. He was only a stone's throw from the woman's house. But he needed backup. In his pocket was a remote with GPS tracking. He pressed the button and waited a second before a short, bald man dressed in brown monk's robes appeared in front of him. The teleporter was one of the best in the world and had a deep-seated grudge against the gods. The perfect ally.

"This better be good. I was with our leader."

"I need to get into her house to see if anything's changed. They have cameras, but I know where they are."

The bald man nodded and held out his hand. "Think of the place."

He did just that and the next thing he knew, he was standing in the corner of her living room where the tiny cameras wouldn't see him. He applauded his own intelligence for finding them so easily.

Dogs barked outside, but in the middle of the day no one was around to hear them. He searched quickly for any sign that would indicate her association to the gods or Deities who ruled on earth. The bald man waited patiently, his eyes closed to conserve every ounce of energy.

Minutes into his search he felt the pressure of a mighty Olympian aura. His time was up. "Let's go."

He reached for the teleporter and thought about his safe house. They were standing there in the blink of an eye.

"That was a close call. Do not attempt such a risk again," the teleporter scolded him. "I'm much too valuable to the cause." Another blink and he was gone.

Arrogant bastard, he thought. Too bad it was true. But soon he would be valuable to the leaders too. Once he killed the girl, exposed her for what she was, the rogues would exalt him as well.

Avery sat in her living room, her heeled shoe tapping nervously on the hardwood. It was eight o'clock and her cell hadn't rung all afternoon. Upon returning home from work, she'd showered, fixed her hair, put on a sexy dress, and even dug her high heels out of the closet. By seven, she had checked her cell phone to make sure it was charged. She'd called Izzy just to see if the damn thing worked. And now she sat—staring at it—waiting.

It never rang.

She let in her two dogs, Castor and Pollux, so she could feed and play with them to pass the time. The German Shepherds were happy to see their master. She didn't mind the dog hair on her dress. If Ryse didn't like dogs, they didn't have a snowball's chance in—

What the hell was she thinking? The jerk hadn't even called! Who gave a rat's ass if he liked dogs?

By ten, she stomped to her bedroom and threw the heels back into the closet. *Damn jerk.* This was what she got for putting herself out there. A man as good looking as Ryse could have any woman he wanted. Why would he waste his time on her? Avery was an overworked, overstressed woman of—a certain unnameable age—who usually smelled like a kitchen and hadn't had a real boyfriend since fourth grade when a freckled-face Frank shoved a potted plant in her hands and said "My mom told me to give this to you." That was the extent of her relationship knowledge.

Yep, she was a real catch. No wonder he didn't call.

At ten-fifteen her cell phone rang and she jumped over her couch with the skill of a gold medalist to answer it. The dogs ran behind her, thinking she was playing. When she read the name on the screen, her heart fell.

"Hi Frank." She walked back to her room, swatted Castor's nose when he nipped at her ankle, still wanting to play.

"Hey kiddo. Didn't figure you'd be up."

"I was just going to bed," Avery lied as she unzipped her dress and let it slip to the floor.

"Tomorrow your day off?"

"Yeah. I plan on sleeping in so don't bug me," Avery teased and she could hear Frank chuckle. She made him hold long enough to slip on a camisole. "Can I ask you something?"

"Sure."

"Am I hot?"

Whatever Frank had been drinking got caught in his throat. He choked and coughed. "Where the hell did that come from? You nearly made me spew my beer."

Avery flopped down on the bed and put her arm over her eyes. "I just mean, if you weren't like my freakin' brother, would you think I'm attractive?" The dogs jumped up with her and licked her face and arm. At least these guys loved her.

There was a long pause on the other end of the phone. "Uh, Avery, it might break this platonic code we got goin' on, but I think you're the prettiest damn thing this side of the Mississippi."

Leave it to Frank to heal the bruises on her heart. Why couldn't she be attracted to him? It would make her life so simple.

But you don't want simple, do you? asked a small voice in the back of her mind.

"So if you were to ask me out, you wouldn't forget to call me and cancel?"

Frank let out a heavy breath. "Hell. I see. Who is he?"

"It's no big deal. I just met him today."

"Brenden's friend? That underwear model lookin' guy?"

Avery chuckled and told him about their meeting. He teased when she told him how she'd dropped the mug and banged her head on the table.

"It sounds really stupid, but I thought we had a connection."

"You don't ever have connections," Frank stated with a hint of sour grapes in his tone.

Avery stood and paced her room while she vented. "I know. But I felt something, Frank. I can't explain it. He acted like he really wanted to go out with me. Jeez. I'm so gullible. What a joke, right? Did you see him? Izzy called him a walking orgasm inducer."

"Hold that thought, I have to vomit," Frank deadpanned.

Avery laughed. She was probably talking to the wrong person. "You don't want to hear this. I'm sorry."

"Naw, it's fine. He sure was a tall sucker. No stranger to the gym. I guess you think he was shit on a stick, huh?"

Avery giggled. "Yeah, Frank. Something like that." She paused, remembering the way her breath had stilled in her lungs when Ryse smiled. Then she rubbed her hand over her heart that now ached with his rejection. "This is why I never date. It hurts too much to risk it."

"Wow kiddo, you really wanted to see this guy."

She could hear the bewilderment in his voice.

"I'm tired of being alone, Frank. I know I have you but . . ." She couldn't say what she wanted to in fear of hurting his feelings.

"I get it Avery. We're not strangers to this conversation. You need a guy that trips your trigger."

"I need a guy that can pick up the freaking phone. That way I'm not sitting at the house all night waiting on him like a schmuck."

"Aw, give him some slack. I'm sure he had a good reason."

Avery stopped pacing and examined her face in the mirror. She rarely wore makeup. Tonight her eyes were smoky with shadow, her cheeks pink, and lips red with gloss. Efforts spent on a man who didn't even call. "Honestly Frank, I don't give a damn to hear it."

She washed the makeup off her face, put her hair in a braid, and curled up with her pillow, the dogs sleeping at the foot of her bed. At least Castor and Pollux would never leave her. She went to sleep wishing she could get the color of Ryse's eyes out of her head. What else had she expected from a man like that? He probably had women in every state and two in Texas. There was no room in her life for a player.

Her heart was too valuable—and too vulnerable.

Frank rolled over at five a.m. to see who the blue blazes was calling him. "Billings here."

"Frank, forgive the early hour. But I need to speak with you."

The minute he heard that voice, he knew. This was the muscled dirt bag who hurt his best friend. "You've got some balls calling me." Frank sat up and scrubbed a hand down his face.

"I am deeply sorry and I plan to make it up to her, you have my word."

"You want to make it up to her? Never show your face in that café again, alright?"

"I'm afraid I can't do that Frank."

"You'd better try. She waited all damned night on you. If you think she's one of these flunkies that will fall into bed with you, you might as well pack up and move on."

"I am aware that Avery is a woman of integrity. It is not my intention to get her to—fall into bed with me, as you put it. I would try to court her properly."

His language caught Frank off guard. Who the hell talks like that in Texas? "You're not from around here, are ya?"

"No, Frank. I'm not." There was humor in his voice.

Something tugged in the back of Frank's mind. It was something Avery had said the day he'd found her cowered in a corner of her living room. She'd been wrapped in a blanket, her clothes covered in blood. Two men had broken into her home, raped her, beat her up, and left as quickly and mysteriously as they came. She'd been twenty at the time. The police had no leads, no forensic evidence left behind from the attackers, and no idea how they could have covered their tracks so thoroughly.

"They said I was no good to them now. They wouldn't come for me because I was impure."

At the time it was gibberish mumbled from the mouth of a hysteric woman. For some reason, Frank had a hunch this proper talking stranger and that attack were connected. But was this a friend or foe?

"What are your intentions, son?" Frank hated how much he sounded like an old man the instant the words crossed his lips. How many times had his father asked that of his sister's boyfriends?

There was low laughter on the other end of the line. "It's been a long time since anyone but my father has called me son." He paused. "I have only her best interests at heart. You have my word. I have regrettably disappointed her and I will right this situation, with or without your help. But it would expedite the process if I have your permission to pursue her. Your opinion means a great deal. I would never want you to feel uneasy about my actions toward her."

Yep, this joker was something out of this world. His gut churned and Frank knew that something monumental was about to happen to his best friend. For most of their adult life, he'd been her go-to guy. He might not have a ring on her finger, but she belonged to him. He'd bought her two German Shepherds and those dogs were like their kids.

Yet, the one time he and Avery had kissed in a romantic way, there had been no spark—at least not for her. She was waiting for something, for someone who would change her world. Frank's biggest fear was that she would find a man to do just that.

He pinched his eyes together, gritted his teeth and took a deep breath. What if this was the guy? This one was different. What if he was the man who made Avery complete in a way Frank couldn't?

"Damn it. I can't believe I'm doing this. You don't deserve her, you'd better get that through your skull real quick."

"I know."

"If you want to get in Avery's good graces, here's what you do." Frank told Ryse the secrets to winning Avery's favor. When their conversation was over, Frank stared at the dead phone. Ryse had promised to protect her before hanging up. It was an odd choice of words, but Frank knew that was exactly what Avery needed.

CHAPTER THREE

"I'M COMING!" AVERY yelled as she threw on her robe to answer the front door. Castor and Pollux were barking and her head hurt like hell. It might have been from crying herself to sleep the night before, but she wouldn't admit it.

Today was her only day off all week. Whoever had awakened her at six in the morning better be bleeding or have the last name Depp.

When she opened the door, her body froze. Standing there in all his beauty and glory was Ryse. Jeans and black cotton had never turned her on so quickly. Then she remembered sitting by the phone all night and her chest ached again. Only when she recalled that pain did she look away, her jaws clenched up.

"What are you doing here?" she bit out, hiding her body behind the door.

"About last night, something came up and I couldn't—"

"Save it. I don't care. I lived a perfectly happy life before you blew into town and I'll live the same happy life after you're gone." She tried to shut the door, but Ryse stopped it.

He held out a bundle of blue roses. They were the most exquisite things Avery had ever beheld. Where on earth did he buy blue roses before six in the morning?

"Please," he begged. "I'm truly sorry I hurt you."

Avery didn't move. She didn't know if she could. He actually regretted ditching her?

Ryse stepped forward and slowly touched her cheek. "Let me in?"

Why did it seem he was asking entrance to much more than her house? His eyes peered straight into her soul and warmth spread over her body. Again she inhaled his scent and quivered. Her physical being was magnetically drawn to him. Everything in her mind relaxed and she felt safe. Her eyes veered down to his lips.

Perfect. They called to her, begging to be kissed until her body leaned in a fraction.

Castor and Pollux barked, demanding attention. It was just the snap back to reality she needed. Ryse was a drug and she required a serious detox. He bent down and addressed the dogs. They came quickly to his outstretched hand, vying for his affections. Avery gave Ryse their names and he shot his eyes to her face.

"Interesting choice."

"They were gods or something. I read about them. Thought they were unique." Avery crossed her arms over her chest, suddenly remembering she was in nothing but a camisole and a robe. "Look, why don't you call me later and—"

"I brought food. Ingredients, actually." He rose to his full height and turned to reveal grocery bags sitting on the porch behind him. "I heard you're a phenomenal chef and you favored breakfast."

Damn it. Someone had informed him. "And what little birdie told you that?"

He had the decency to give her a sheepish grin as he tugged on the collar of his shirt. "Frank."

"Frank?" Avery blanched. Well, wasn't that a shift in the fabric of the universe? Last night Frank had been ready to rip Ryse's head off.

"Will you make me leave hungry, Avery?" He peered at her under those thick lashes and her insides softened. He was playing dirty.

Frank would pay for this.

She narrowed her eyes and her lips thinned into a straight line. "You set things out in the kitchen while I get dressed." She poked him in the chest. "Don't make me regret trusting you a second time."

There was no way this could end well, and yet she showed him to the kitchen where he unloaded groceries. Never had she dressed so quickly. Her hair was still braided and she let it be. There was no time to tame the wild mass of brown curls. Before she entered the kitchen, she took a deep breath and prayed she wasn't setting herself up for another heartache.

Ryse could feel her unease as she came back into the room. Her movements didn't betray her though. Avery was the master of her kitchen and she shooed him out of the way.

He had to make amends. Last night had been unavoidable. Once he and his men returned to their makeshift headquarters, Cutter, who stayed behind to keep eyes on Avery, made Ryse watch the video from her house. Seeing Avery pace around her house in that sexy black dress had killed him inside. When she finally gave up and went to sleep, Ryse could barely stomach himself. He'd disappointed her. Whatever it took, he would make it up to her. Even if he crossed every line there was.

"So," she said curtly. "What was so important you had to blow me off?"

Well, well. She wasn't going to give a man an inch, was she? Ryse was ready with a partially fabricated alibi. He sat down at the bar and watched her work.

"I don't know if Brenden told you why I'm here, but I'm a bounty hunter of sorts."

She raised a brow in his direction.

"The department called in my team because they believed a serial killer is in the area. We've been chasing him; we're familiar with this M.O. Last night we came close to catching him. It was time consuming."

"Who's he after, cows? Cause that's about all there is around here."

"Young women between the ages of twenty and thirty," Ryse said with a hard tone so she would know he was serious. He wasn't about to tell her that the trail he and his men followed last night came within three hundred yards of her house then appeared clear across town.

He also didn't presume this was a good time to say the bounty he was after wasn't completely human. Minor detail.

Her face fell. "Oh." The message was received. Being as stubborn as she was, she still wasn't going to let it slide. "They have phones at the station, you know. There's not an officer up there that doesn't have my number."

Ryse shook his head. "You're not going to let me off easy, are you?"

She turned around and put one hand on her hip. In her other hand was a knife. "Why should I? Do you have any idea how hard it is to be a female business owner in this town? Sometimes I feel like I live in the Wild West, not modern day Texas. Men 'round here either call me 'sugar' with sexism drippin' off their tongues or they think I'm some kinda he-woman. The pool is limited. I don't accept date offers from anyone, but I did from you and look what I got back."

Gods have mercy, she was beautiful when she was riled up. And that accent! How was he supposed to resist such a strong woman? What had Frank advised? She's used to being in control. Say things that throw her off balance.

"You're incredibly intimidating when you are angry and holding a cleaver. It's attractive."

It must have worked. Avery's eyes widened before she blushed and turned back to the ingredients sitting on her counter top. "Don't say things like that, especially if you're just blowing smoke up my skirt. I don't need pretty words. I need sincere actions."

Ryse laughed. "Heavens woman! I can't compliment you. I can't apologize. Will you not allow me to make amends at all? I'll beg." He threw his hands up in the air and they fell to his knees with a *slap.*

Immediately Castor and Pullox came over and sniffed him, wanting to play. "See, they forgive me. Don't you boys?" He scratched their heads and gave them a good rub. "Dogs have an uncanny sense about people. You can't argue with it."

Avery rolled her eyes and pink colored her cheeks. "They also chase their own tails. They're not the brightest bulbs on the tree."

Ryse gasped and covered Castor's ears. "She didn't mean it, boy," he whispered to the pooch.

She tried not to, but she laughed. Ryse stood right in front of her. She looked up to his face. The laughter stopped and she swallowed hard.

"I apologize." He took her face in his hands and kissed her right cheek. She sucked in a breath; her body trembled. He moved to her other cheek. "I'm sorry." He kissed her forehead. "I'm an inconsiderate jerk. I plead for forgiveness." Then he shocked the poor girl and gently kissed her lips.

Sensation threatened to drown him. He could taste the mint of her toothpaste, the sweetness of her skin. She smelled of fruit and sugar and something much more carnal. It was all he could do not to deepen the kiss, flick out his tongue, and demand entrance to her mouth.

May the gods help him, he had no idea it would be this way. All his life he'd avoided physical contact with others. Given his occupation, it was easier that way. But Avery's inspiriting presence had him breaking all his personal rules. Kissing her was his greatest gift and his greatest mistake.

Before his body could overrule his brain, he pulled back. The whimper she let out nearly brought him to his knees. Her chest moved up and down with every short breath and her eyes remained closed even after he pulled away.

"Do you forgive me?" Ryse whispered against her lips.

"Uh-huh." The entranced response made him smile.

Avery clutched the countertop behind her so hard her knuckles were white. Ryse reached down and took her hands, massaging the blood back into them. He used a tiny fraction of his aura to warm her fingers. Avery studied his face.

"You should put those flowers in water, love." When she continued to stare at him, he thought he'd made a mistake by kissing her. "What?"

"You shouldn't have this effect on me."

Curiosity ate him alive. "What do you mean?" He stepped back to give her room. Ryse made sure his aura was locked up tight. Giving himself away could be a problem. Avery had no idea what he was and he didn't want to tip her off. His pulse spiked in anticipation of her answer.

Did she sense him after all?

CHAPTER FOUR

IN THE LAST fifteen minutes, she had run the emotional gamut. Ryse was overwhelming to be around. First she was pissed, then shocked, then excited and now she wanted to put a lot of distance between them before she jumped him like a horny teenager. There was something so familiar about his presence. It spoke to her of companionship and desire. It made her believe she could trust him.

Avery didn't trust anyone.

She turned her back. "I don't know anything about you."

"But?"

"But nothin.' I don't know you and you're standin' in my kitchen kissin' me stupid. And I know you've been talkin' in depth to Frank because only he knows my favorite breakfast." Avery held up two packages of cheese. "Ricotta and asiagio. Nobody buys both on the fly."

Ryse took the hint and sat back down behind her bar. He'd certainly been coached because the ingredients for her special avocado omelets were in the bag. Frank knew her favorites. Only Frank.

"He might have mentioned a thing or two."

"Why?" Avery got to work on the flowers. She snipped the ends and put the roses in water. The aroma of the flowers was comforting. "Frank usually points a gun at men who show interest in me."

"Perhaps he has good taste, or faith."

Ha! The only thing Frank had faith in was his sidearm.

"Well, I need to have a talk with him about stickin' his nose in my business either way." she mumbled, secretly pleased Frank had put aside his feeling for her and given Ryse a chance. He really was a good man. Guilt pinged her heart.

"Avery?" Ryse called for her attention. "Are you okay over there?

"Yeah, sorry." She busied her hands preparing food. "Why don't you tell me about yourself so I don't feel like a total stranger is sittin' in my kitchen?"

Ryse smiled, causing her heart to sputter. Avery cooked him breakfast while they volleyed facts about themselves. Ryse was easy to talk to. He seemed genuinely interested in how she inherited the café and house, about how her parents passed away and all the disasters that followed.

His parents were still living and in some sort of political position. He had a brother who was a historian. Years ago he'd gotten into law enforcement and the progression to bounty hunter was a swift one.

When Avery set the plate in front of him, he scooped up a bite. "I'm in love," he mumbled around the food.

It gave her great pride when he moaned and his eyes closed. She loved to feed people and have others enjoy her food. But watching Ryse savor the meal was a religious experience. And she could be a devout follower to that religion.

He finished his breakfast in half the time it took her. When he asked, for seconds she happily complied.

Finally, he leaned back in his chair and slapped his swollen belly. "I feel the need for a nap. Wow."

"Would you like some coffee?" Avery jumped up to fix him a cup, delighted to take care of him.

"You don't have to—" There was already a hot steaming mug in his hands. "Thank you, Avery. You're an amazing chef."

When he looked up at her, she caught a flash in his eyes, something like a spark that lit, then vanished quickly.

"It's nothing." She shrugged. The way he smiled had her heart fluttering like hummingbird wings.

For a moment she let herself think of what it'd be like to replay this scene every morning. They could spend Saturdays drinking coffee and eating delicious food she'd prepared. Perhaps it'd be after a night of making love. They could go for long walks with the dogs, curl up together on cold winter days. Would he sleep naked on those hot Texas nights?

Shit. She forced herself to turn away from the entrapment of those thoughts. That would never happen because he was only in town for a job. By Monday, if he was any good, he'd be gone and hunting some other criminal, leaving her heartbroken and alone.

"You enjoy taking care of people, don't you?" he asked, bringing her back to the here-and-now.

The skin on her face heated. She gave a casual shrug. "Yeah, I guess so. Food is my forte, you know? I like knowin' people are full and healthy. It's my superpower." It felt silly, now that she'd said it, but it was true. He nodded as if he understood exactly what she meant.

Time for a subject change.

"How long are you in town for?" That topic would bring her back to reality.

Ryse's brows dipped low and he stared at his coffee. "I'm not sure."

"Do you make friends like this everywhere you go? Find a woman to cook for you while you're not home?" Avery was teasing, but the deepening scowl on his face indicated he didn't find it humorous.

"No. I'm usually more of an introvert. I rarely speak to anyone but my crew when I have to go out on a job."

"I find that hard to believe. A man with your charm surely has women at his disposal."

He tilted his head up and narrowed his eyes. "Women shouldn't be for anyone's disposal. If a man can't act honorably to a woman, he should stay the hell away from her to begin with."

"Says the man who stood me up." Avery flashed a cocky grin.

"That's it." Ryse popped out of his chair and made a grab for Avery. Anticipating his movements, she dodged and ran into the living room.

Her heart pounded in her chest. Something about Ryse chasing her was sexy and exciting. She laughed as they went back and forth around the couch. Finally, he jumped it and wrapped a muscular arm around her waist. Avery giggled and kicked as he pulled her down on the cushions. Ryse was merciless as he tickled and pinched her, finally ending up on top of her.

The giggles and laughter slowly faded, replaced by something deeper and hotter. Avery felt a flicker in her core. It was soft, a match striking to light in a place that had been cast in darkness her whole life. Warmth spread over her body until she could feel beads of sweat on her forehead. When Ryse lowered his body over hers, she stared at his lips.

Please kiss me. Please kiss me. For the love of all that's holy, please kiss me.

Her wish was fulfilled. Ryse's lips descended onto hers and the flame within burned slightly brighter.

Usually Avery never would've been so bold as to reach under his shoulders and pull his body closer to her, but Ryse ripped through her inhibitions. Their lips mingled and when he dipped his tongue into her mouth, she didn't hold back. The taste of him had her moaning. Coffee and Ryse combined into pure ambrosia. He slid his hand down her thigh and brought her leg up over his hip. She managed to keep from rubbing her body against him by an impressive feat of willpower.

Naturally, her dogs would choose that moment to come sniffing around. Just as Ryse was making his way to the curve of her bottom, Avery felt a cold nose at her ear and a slobbery tongue on her cheek.

"Oh! Pullox!"

Ryse chuckled and moved over so Avery could wipe the slime off her face.

"I was hoping that wasn't you," she teased Ryse.

"I don't think I drool that badly." Ryse looked down at her and cocked a brow. "I do have to say, you look very sexy all disheveled." Her shirt was pushed upwards, nearly exposing her chest, and her hair was escaping the braid, curls springing out everywhere. She could feel the heat in her face and her lips were wet.

Avery straightened her clothes. "It's probably a good thing we were interrupted. I seem to have *no* self-control around you."

Ryse stood up and turned his back to adjust himself. "You're telling me."

"Don't you have a criminal to catch? I'm keeping you from your work." She nervously smoothed down the mess of her hair. Now if she could slow down her pulse.

"My team is working on some leads. They will call if they have anything of use."

Avery nodded and searched for something in the room to look at, anything but the attractive man in front of her.

"Might I inquire about how you and Frank became so close?" Ryse sat back down on the edge of the couch as if he didn't want to get too close to her.

"Frank?" Why would he bring up Frank at such an awkward moment? "We went to school together. My parents were killed in a car accident right after we graduated. Frank was in police training and since he was the only guy that knew me, they made him come with the officer on duty to deliver the news. Since then," she said, shrugging and thinking of how close Frank had become, "he's been my best friend. Even more than Izzy in some ways."

"Why haven't you settled down with him?"

Avery blanched. The thought was preposterous. Frank was more of a brother. "Frank is a good man. And I love him." She shook her head, bunching up her shoulders. "But the spark isn't there. Not like—" She snapped her mouth shut before she dug a hole she couldn't get out of. "There's nothing but friendship there."

It was time to get off this subject—*quick.*

"What about you? No wife and kids two states away thinkin' Daddy will be home soon?"

"You have a mean streak in you, do you know that?" Ryse's lips kicked up and it had a direct effect on her pulse. "What was that phrase you used earlier? You 'kiss me stupid' *then* ask if I'm married?"

"You never know these days." Avery wasn't about to apologize for being cynical. Even in her small town there were as many unfaithful as there were faithful. Truth be told, it was hard to believe Ryse hadn't been scooped up multiple times.

"I promise, no wife. No kids. No romantic connections of any type."

"So you're a player who's afraid of commitment?"

"Not hardly. There are numerous things and people I am devoted to."

Avery tilted her head to the side, squinting. "Mama's boy?"

"Every man should respect his mother—from a distance when necessary."

"Good answer." Damn, was there anything wrong with him? "You're not secretly gay are you? 'Cause that would put a damper on how this relationship goes from here. You do have great hair—and you are really pretty."

Ryse barked out a laugh and hauled her into his lap. "I'll let you figure that out right now." He kissed her hard and deep. Their tongues danced together with passion she'd never known. Under her bunched fist she could feel a rapid heartbeat. It matched the rhythm of her own. Her body came alive once more, searching and needing something from him. More—she simply wanted more.

Avery spoke against his lips, just to tease him. "That was almost convincing."

Ryse laughed and swatted her rump before connecting their lips again.

A wave of heat rolled through her, all the way down to her bones. What was this? Why did she react to a complete stranger the way most would react to a well-known lover? It went against every rule in her life, pushed every boundary. And yet, she couldn't stop.

Ryse pulled back his head in a rush and took a deep breath. "We should, ah, do something . . . else for a while." His brows dipped low on his face, his nostrils flared, and his jaw tightened.

Avery moved off him, self-conscious about his abrupt retreat. "Right."

Why had he stopped? Was she a bad kisser? It's not like she was experienced. Maybe he knew that? God, could she please find a hole to crawl into?

"What do you usually do on your day off?" Ryse asked as he folded a small blanket that had been kicked around during their kissing. Avery watched in wonder as he placed it lovingly on the back of her couch. Mercy, she could get used to seeing him in her home.

"I do chores. I know, it's a very exciting lifestyle I lead. But it takes a lot to keep this place up."

Ryse nodded and pushed up the sleeves of his shirt. His forearms were distractingly thick. No human should be so toned. "What's first?"

"Huh?" she asked in a moment of brilliance.

"Chores. Exciting household stuff. You made breakfast; I might as well repay you by being useful."

At a loss for words, Avery crinkled up her nose and shook her head. "I don't think you need to be helping with laundry and flower-beds." She stood to busy herself by tidying up an already clean house. There were a lot of things she needed to get done, but it felt odd with Ryse there.

Flashing a grin that could dissolve all her barriers, he ran a finger down her cheek. "You have a strong male here that's willing to do some heavy lifting. Take advantage of me."

Mother of all things holy, could she ever. Her brain wasn't used to being fried so often. Ryse was dangerous in every way. How many times had he left her unable to move and think already? If she didn't get a grip on her higher motor skills, he was going to break her in every way possible.

She cleared her throat and looked away. "I do have a tree limb that's hangin' precariously close to the house. Frank said he was going to cut it down, but then Brenden came on board at the station and he's forgotten—"

"Consider it done." Ryse asked where her tools were and went outside.

Avery went to her room and collapsed on her bed. She was seriously going to fall for this guy and that was a horrible thing. He's going to leave, she kept repeating in her head. He's going to leave. Don't be stupid McClain. Men like that don't stick around.

Yet here he was, cutting down a limb over her porch. After that was done, she couldn't stand the thought of him taking care of her home. It produced too many fantasies. She suggested a long walk to let the dogs run. Once again, Ryse amazed her as he played fetch with the boys. The damn dogs minded him better than they did her. When it began to sprinkle, they headed back inside.

Avery fixed Ryse a gourmet lunch that received his praises. Watching him bring in firewood created an odd sense of home. Could she ever convince him to stick around for a while after his job was done?

How nice it would be to spend every day doing such domestic things with a man by her side. Especially Ryse. She loved the way his body moved under his shirt, the way his black hair fell in his face. And she adored the way he devoured her home-cooked meal.

They curled up on the couch for an afternoon siesta.

"You love this place, don't you?" Ryse asked, his fingers moving up and down on her arm.

Now was her chance to make things clear for him—and to see how he reacted. "More than most people understand. It's my home; it was my parent's home. My father built that kitchen just for my mother. She taught me to cook. When I use the same recipes and pans, work in the same space she used to work in, I feel connected to her."

Ryse was quiet for a long moment. "What if the right guy came along and asked you to run away with him?"

Avery sat up and looked him square in the eyes. "If he's the right guy, he would know not to ask."

The deep scowl on his face bothered her. Talk about ending something before it ever began.

"The thing is, Ryse, this is the town I grew up in, my parents are buried here, my whole life is here. I love the cafe. It's a piece of my mom. I love this house and this ranch because it's a piece of my dad. It might not be ideal, but I'm happy—right here."

That last part was a partial lie. She was content, for sure. She had her life: the cafe, her friends, her routine. But something had always been missing, even when her parents were alive. Deep in the recesses of her soul, buried away, was a voice that told her she wasn't destined to live her life in this small town. It was that voice that said no to every dinner date, every invitation for coffee, and every kind smile . . . until Ryse. And that scared her.

Ryse wasn't the kind of man to stick around in a tiny Texas town. His job kept him mobile and was full of adventure. He'd told her as much. Maybe they would have a couple steamy nights together, maybe he would call after he left, maybe not. The idea of him leaving caused a sick feeling in her stomach.

When his phone went off, he apologized and went into the next room to take the call. She didn't understand some of what was said, but she got the point of the conversation.

"I'm afraid I have to go, baby. Duty calls." He held her face in his hands. "Can I come back later?" Deep brown eyes begged for permission. Was there any other answer but yes? Even if it broke her heart later, was he worth the risk?

"I'm going out tonight," she remembered out loud. "But you're welcome to come. Marshall's Bar, over by the interstate, at seven."

"I'll try my best to be there." He kissed her hard and long. It was a promise.

"It's okay if you can't come. You can meet me back here—if you want." Truth was, she wasn't willing to give up on any kind of relationship with him, even if it did end as quickly as it began. The thought of waking up to him after a night of tangling in the sheets was so alluring it stunned her. Ryse was the first man she'd ever extended that offer to.

"Yes," he said quickly. Ryse picked her up and sat her on the kitchen countertop. Then he overtook her mouth in a carnal and feral kiss that made her whole body awaken. By the time he pulled away, her arms were around his neck, her hands clenching his hair, and her lips pulsed with the sting where he nipped at her. "I'll come back to you. I swear it. Be careful tonight."

As Ryse sped out of the driveway, Avery's knees went slack. She closed her front door and fell into a chair at her kitchen table. "What the hell is it about that man?" she asked the empty house. Castor and Pullox tilted their heads, watching her talk to herself. "I know, I'm actin' squirrel shit nutty."

Avery shook her head and tried to clear the fog. Ryse was the kind of man her mama had warned her about. The kind that would take her heart fast and break her heart faster.

CHAPTER FIVE

RYSE GAPED AT the wall in front of him and felt nauseated. Pictures of Avery were everywhere. The lair of the rogue held evidence of his obsession. Years upon years worth of research into one woman's life was tacked and taped onto the wood. There were pictures of her parents and her friends, candid photos they never knew were taken. Articles about her parent's car accident, about her rape and assault, mementos from her house and café. Whoever this bastard was, he knew Avery's every movement.

"Master." Yankee snapped his fingers in front of Ryse's face. "You should calm down, man. You're doing that light bulb shit again," he said, referring to the way Ryse's body glowed when he used the powers of the gods. It took a lot of willpower not to destroy this place.

"I want him caught and killed, do you understand me?" His voice had gone rough and deep. "No questions, just kill him."

"We are all working on it, boss. But this guy, he's no rookie. Whoever he is, he's stayed off the radar." Yankee went back to examining the stalker wall.

Hammon came to stand beside him. "His aura is very tightly shielded. I don't sense him in this place, and yet there is no doubt he has spent much time here. A powerful magic controls him. There are signs of darkness everywhere." Hammon pointed out various tools of witchcraft. The stalker had used the blood of small animals to put wards over the windows and doors. The blood of innocents made the magic stronger.

But the wards were old. He had gotten comfortable and slacked off. It was a good thing. If those wards had been fresh, Hammon might not have sensed his aura.

"Are we sure it's a man?" Ryse asked as he picked up a picture of Avery and a group of women laughing together.

"Yes," Bren said without hesitation. His years of police expertise were their best ally in this situation. "Look at these pictures. They are . . . intimate, romantic even. This is not just a job to him anymore. He's consumed. I don't think he is too close to her though. Everything is from a distance. If I had to profile, I would say someone that only comes in brief contact when he needs a fix. I'll start looking at handymen, service repair guys that might work at the café when needed."

Ryse picked up a picture of Avery's parents. "Someone that has been around for a while. Who owns this house?"

"The city," Philippe answered in Italian. "It was abandoned a few years ago and they took ownership. I'll get records on every city employee."

The men noted everything they could about the lair and installed a microscopic camera in the corner. The next person who came through the door would be caught, the video sent to Ryse's cell phone. Modern technology had its uses.

On their drive back to base, Yankee leaned over with his shit-eating grin. "So did she forgive you for being a dick last night?"

"She was not pleased." Ryse looked over at the mouthy warrior. "But yes, after a verbal lashing, I'm back in her good graces. I'm seeing her again tonight."

"My oh my, the mighty Master Ryse has fallen—for a country girl at that." Yankee shook his head and chuckled.

Yes, Ryse thought, I have most definitely fallen for a country girl.

As Izzy came through the front door, she called out, "Avery, where are you, woman?"

"In here!" she called out from her bathroom. Avery brushed more shadow on her eyes and checked her lipstick.

"Are you ready to—hot damn!" Izzy let out a whistle when she saw Avery dressed up for their night out. "Honey, the only thing you're missing is a line across your forehead that says 'must be this tall to ride.' Who're you trying to impress?"

Avery smoothed down the lacy ruffles of the white dress. She loved the way it shaped her body, but still flowed when she danced. "Ryse said he might come."

"Frank told me that he stood you up? I thought we were pissed at him?"

"You and Frank gossip like old women. I forgave him. He had a good reason."

Izzy shook her head. "He's sexy. You can forgive a sexy guy a lot."

Avery rolled her eyes. Izzy would let a guy walk all over her if there was a promise of hot makeup sex later.

"He's more than just a sexy guy, Izz." She took a deep breath and put a hand on her chest. "He's amazing. He's charming and funny and yeah, he makes me want to crawl all over him. But there's something deeper, you know? Something so *right* about being around him."

Izzy flopped down in a chair and grinned, her bright red lipstick showing off her lustrous smile. "Sister, you marry him if you want to. As long as I get to hump his leg every now and then." She wiggled her eyebrows.

"Izzy!"

The two women giggled. Usually Avery had to listen to Izzy's stories. But tonight she had a couple to tell. When she showed Izzy the blue roses, her friend's mouth fell open.

"Does he have a brother?"

"He does."

"Well, hot damn! If he's half as sexy as Ryse, I'll send their parents a card that says thank you and well done." They giggled again. "Here, let me fix your hair." Izzy came to stand behind her. She wrapped her arms around Avery's shoulders and smiled at her in the mirror. "I'm really happy for you." Avery leaned into her hold. Izzy wasn't serious that often. "I hope this guy brings you some happiness, girl. It's about time something wonderful happened to you."

Avery's heart sputtered. Izzy wasn't a sentimental person, so this heartfelt gesture meant the world to her.

As they drove over to Marshall's Bar, she tried not to get her hopes up. Ryse only promised to try to show up. Even if they didn't get to spend time together with her friends, he had sworn he'd come over later. Avery prayed he kept his word this time.

The bar was crowded that Saturday night. Avery's first thought was that she'd dressed too provocatively. Men stared at her as she walked over to the table where Jerry, Brenden, and Frank sat. They were surrounded by off-duty officers and dispatch workers.

It was the table everyone else in the bar was avoiding.

Loud country music boomed over the speakers and couples danced around the sawdust-covered floor. People were laughing and drinking, having a good time, but Avery was a nervous wreck. If he did show, Ryse would stand out like a sore thumb in a place like this. There was something too *refined* about him.

"Hey baby girl! You look sweet as honey." Jerry picked her up and swung her around. He flashed a bright smile that had been the undoing of many women in town. "Might have to get me a taste of that."

Avery giggled. "Silly man, put me down."

"Come on, dance with me." He pulled her out on the floor and swung her around with professional skill.

Despite her nerves, Avery enjoyed the hell out of it. Jerry was the kind of guy you wanted to go dancing with. He could make a woman with two left feet move the right way. An adorable grin stretched across his face, his eyes lit up and creased on the sides. Even when Avery nearly slipped, he twirled her around, held her close and played it off.

By the time they went back to the table, they were both out of breath and laughing about her near face-plant into a wooden beam. Frank sat in the corner. He gave a slight smile that didn't reach his eyes. He would never admit his jealousy; he was better than that.

However, when a slow song played, he took Avery's hand before Jerry could offer. She noticed Izzy had latched on to Brenden and was pulling him up to dance. If he played his cards—at all—he would get lucky.

"I guess that pretty boy showed up at your house, huh?" Frank asked as they swayed to the music.

"Imagine my surprise when he named an accomplice," Avery muttered as she rested her head on his shoulder.

"Don't know what you're talkin' about. I don't even like him."

Avery looked up at Frank's hazel eyes. "Then why?"

Wide shoulders moved up and down once. "He seemed remorseful. Had to have been if he called me. I do own a gun."

That made her smile. Frank had always been her protector, even when she didn't want one. Since her parent's death, Frank had carried an unwarranted guilt.

It had multiplied when he pulled his squad car up in her driveway eight years ago and heard her screaming inside the house. Avery had been curled up in a corner, naked and bleeding between her legs. Her body vibrated from the shock and bruises already forming beneath her skin. She remembered the look on Frank's face, the horror and disbelief. Within minutes the ambulance arrived. Until they entered the house, Frank had held her in his lap and wrapped her in his jacket.

Those men were never found. They were like wind—here one day, gone the next. State police searched. Local police searched. Nothing. It was as if they had appeared just long enough to rape her, then vanished.

"Avery, sweetie, you okay?" Frank's brows dipped as she focused on the here-and-now.

"Sorry, I zoned out for a moment. What did you say?"

"I said he might be a nice feller, given the chance. Not that I'm happy 'bout it."

With a warm smile, Avery nestled her cheek against his. "Don't worry Frank, you'll always be my best guy."

Avery felt eyes on her. She turned from her group of friends and scanned the room. Maybe she was simply wishing Ryse would show up. But something in the back of her mind told her she was being watched. It wasn't the first time she'd felt it this week.

"C'mon baby girl, let's go dance one more time before they shut the place down." Jerry grinned and held out a hand. Though her feet were killing her, Avery sighed and let him pull her from her chair.

"Take it easy on me, darlin,'" she begged. "These boots were made for walkin,' not dancin.'"

Jerry chuckled and gently put his arm around her. "Okay, I'll have mercy on your feet." They fell into a comfortable rhythm. "You having fun? Been watching the door all night."

She didn't want to upset Jerry, but he was dead on. They only had about an hour left and still no Ryse.

Determined not to be the schmuck waiting up all night again, she focused on Jerry. "I'm having a great time. You know I love going out like this. We always have so much fun."

"Hell yeah we do." He smiled and leaned his cheek on her forehead. "Listen, I wanted to talk to you about something. I don't if now's the right time though."

"Go for it. I'm half buzzed," Avery joked.

"That doesn't help, smart ass," he teased. "I just wanted you to know that I'm worried about you."

Avery jerked her head back. "Me? Why?"

He gave a one-shouldered shrug; his cheeks took on a blush. "Well, you know, Frank and I, we do talk about . . . stuff. And I know you haven't been dating or anything. I flirt—"

"With everyone."

"—but it's different with you, baby girl. I, um, I actually mean it with you."

Avery stared up at his sweet face. What the hell did she say to that? And why did Jerry have to make such a confession the day she and Ryse were—doing whatever she and Ryse were doing? If he stood her up again, they wouldn't be doing shit. But if he showed up at her house later, she wouldn't deny him whatever he wanted. Which made her current situation awkward.

"Jerry, I have a confession. You know I love you like a brother, I do. And heaven knows I wouldn't take our friendship for granted. But there's nothing else there."

He nodded, his blush deepened, his eyes averted. "Yeah, I thought that's how it was. And that's okay, really. I hoped over time you and I could—"

"I've met someone, Jerry."

That got his attention. Hurt blossomed on his face. "How? Who? Do I know him?"

"It's Brenden's friend, the guy that was in the cafe with him yesterday. You should know him, he's a bounty hunter the station called in for a case."

Jerry's expression morphed from a concerned brother to a raging bull. His eyes widened and his nostrils flared.

Did he just snarl at me?

"The station would never call in a *bounty hunter* to help with a case, Avery. We have detectives for investigations. You should know that by now." His tone was hard and demeaning. He stopped their dancing and gripped her shoulders. "What else do you know about him?"

Avery's throat closed up. She'd never seen Jerry upset and this new side of him was frightening. "I—I don't know too much more. He came over for a while, but—"

"He's been to your *house?*" Jerry's voice elevated. "What have Frank and I told you about letting people in your house, Avery? Damn it! Do you have a death wish?"

Avery tried to shrug out of his hold, but his grip was firm. "You're hurting me. Stop it."

"Don't take that attitude with me, Avery. Some stranger waltzes into town and you invite him to your *house.* Didn't you learn your lesson the first time?" Avery flinched at the reprimand. Jerry signed heavily and released her arms. "Damn, Avery. You can't do that shit. What if he hurt you?"

"Jerry." She reached for his hand. "It's okay. I trust him. I might not know too much about him, but we connected, you know? I feel like I've known him my whole life."

"You don't know what you've done, do you?" Jerry whispered as he pinched the bridge of his nose. He reached back and rubbed his neck. "I have to go."

Without another word, Jerry stormed out the side entrance of the bar. Avery stood on the dance floor wondering what the hell just happened. Brenden, Frank, and Izzy questioned Jerry's hasty exit, but she had no answers except he had to be upset that she was seeing someone. It was unlike Jerry to get angry over anything. He was one of the happiest people they knew.

"Maybe he has deeper feelings than any of us thought?" Izzy gave Avery a worried look. "Poor guy."

"Yeah." Avery twisted her fingers in her lap. "Now I feel bad. Should I go after him? I hate the thought of him being angry with me."

"It's too late," Frank nodded towards the door. "Your man is here . . . *Finally.*" He muttered the last word with sarcasm.

Avery glanced over her shoulder and nearly fell out of her chair. Her breath caught and her heart skipped a beat. Izzy's nickname for Ryse was all too accurate. Walking orgasm inducer.

He walked through the door in fitted jeans and a button up shirt. His black hair was slicked back with the exception of a stray strand or two. And he had on boots. Honest to goodness shit-kickers. Avery had never seen a man who wore them so well.

Everyone else disappeared. The only person worth seeing approached her table and she was caught in his spell. Avery was lost to those brown eyes and at that moment she didn't care at all that he was late.

CHAPTER SIX

AVERY STOOD TO greet him. Ryse's footsteps faltered when he saw that white sundress. By the gods, she was magnificent. Rich brown hair fell in unruly curls about her bare shoulders. The ruffles of the dress cut off a few inches above her knees and she wore cowboy boots. Layers of pearls accentuated the deep vee of her dress and the swells of her breasts.

It was her emerald eyes that captured him, though. They were full of female appreciation and he couldn't help but puff out his chest a bit. As much as he needed to find the rogue trying to kill her, he knew that if he let Avery down tonight, there might not be a third chance. His men had assured him that going out for an hour or so wouldn't hurt their search.

It wasn't fair of him to lead Avery on as he had this afternoon. Though his experiences with women could be counted on one finger, he knew Avery intended on going to bed with him. The problem was, he couldn't sleep with her, wouldn't even if she wanted to. It wasn't part of his mission.

Neither were those kisses you shared earlier, but that didn't stop you.

Ryse chided himself for letting things cross a line they never should have approached. Falling for Avery wasn't supposed to happen—not like this, anyway. His plan was laid out and had to be followed.

Get Avery out of here, one way or another. If he had to drag her kicking and screaming, he would.

Unfortunately, it was hard to concentrate on what he should be doing with her dressed like an angel. When she smiled, his heart nearly burst out of his chest.

"You came."

Ryse slipped an arm around her waist and splayed his hand over her lower back. He loved the way she came so willingly into his arms. "I didn't want to disappoint you again." Leaning down to take in her scent, he whispered in her ear, "You look simply delicious. I should haul you out of here right now."

"Fine by me." Emerald eyes danced with invitation and Ryse's knees nearly buckled.

He tried to sense her aura, the hum of energy and lights all Olympians gave off, but it was muffled and strained, buried beneath a layer of protection. Did she know what she was? Could she sense him at all? Would she have any idea why he had to take her? By the gods, he hated the thought of hurting her. But the situation had changed. It was time to think about her safety, not necessarily her momentary comfort.

"Will you come and hang out with my friends?" She bit her lip and he nearly came undone.

"Absolutely." Ryse found himself unable to tell her no. Never in his many years of life had he felt the need to please *anyone* so desperately.

Avery led him to the corner where Frank sat, his face blank as he examined Ryse from head to toe. Frank took a deep breath and rose to his feet.

"Frank," Avery said with affection. "You know Ryse."

Her eyes darted between the two men expectantly. Ryse put his pride aside and gave Frank a wide grin, sticking out his hand. "Frank, nice to see you."

"Yep. You too." Frank shook his hand, glanced over at Avery. "Glad you could make it."

"I'm Izzy, her best friend." People at the table chuckled as Izzy stuck her hand in Ryse's face. "Nice to meet you. I hear you have a brother?"

Everyone laughed and Avery leaned her head on his shoulder.

Taking her away from all this was going to be harder than he expected.

All night Avery had been uneasy and nervous. Then Ryse showed up and everything within her settled. Her feet didn't bother her enough to keep her from dancing with him. She wasn't tired enough to worry about laughing it up with her friends. Frank and Ryse talked football and soon they were engrossed in conversation. Izzy and Bren were dancing. She was flirting, but Bren wasn't giving in as easily as most men would.

The bartender gave last call and Ryse took Avery's hand to dance with her. There was nothing like being in his arms. Ryse was a big man, tall and broad, pure muscle and tantalizing strength. He appeared hard except when she leaned into his body, and the rock gave way. She fit perfectly.

"Have I told you how nice you look?" Avery whispered, unsure of how he would take the compliment.

"Thank you."

She noticed tightness in his voice. "Is everything okay?"

His brows furrowed and his lips pinched together as he looked her in the eyes. "Have you ever—" He stopped, looked over her head like he didn't know what he wanted to say. "Avery, you know you're a special woman, right?"

Avery's shoulders went slack. She knew that tone. Frank had it when he talked about a woman he liked, but didn't want to date. "Where ya goin' with that train, Ryse?"

His hand slipped up to her neck. "My job is almost over. My team has a good lead and we've set the trap. Once we catch him, I—" His lips pinched again.

"You're going to leave," she whispered, her heart ripping to pieces. She closed her eyes, resolving not to cry over a man she'd only known for two days.

"Yes."

Avery nodded, turned her face away. "I figured."

A soft touch lifted her chin so she met his eyes. "Come with me."

"I'm not leaving my home, Ryse. I have too many obligations."

His jaw tightened. "Don't you wonder what's out there, Avery? Haven't you ever felt the need to discover—"

"Can we not talk about this?" Avery interrupted. He was hitting far too close to home. "Let's dance and hold each other and not worry about tomorrow."

Ryse gave a heavy sigh and bent his face to her neck. "Okay, baby."

There was no denying she wanted to be with Ryse. But leaving her house, her cafe, Frank, Jerry, and Izzy? Her entire life had played out in this town. Good or bad, it was home.

The real problem was that, beneath her reasons for staying, she longed to be something more than a waitress, more than a small town girl with small dreams and small possibilities. Her parents had often said once Avery graduated, they would move back to where they'd met. They didn't speak of it much, but Avery had the feeling it was a special place they missed dearly.

So what had kept her in this town?

Fear. The safety of knowing Frank was nearby.

Routine. This was her comfort zone. She knew her place and depended on the predictability of her life.

Ryse's lips touched her neck and shattered her thoughts. If she was so dependent on the comfort zone she'd created, how could this one stranger come in and blow it to pieces?

"Can I come over?" he asked when they were walking out to her car. She leaned back against the door and welcomed his weight when he pinned her there. They had said goodbye to everyone and only Brenden remained. "I have to take him home, but then I'm free."

"Don't keep me waiting." Avery brushed her lips over his and reveled in the electricity that passed between them. As Ryse deepened the kiss, she hitched her leg up, her boot resting against the door. His warm hand traveled under her dress from her knee to her thigh. Just before he cupped her bottom, the horn on his SUV blared and startled them both.

They broke the kiss in a rush of air and panting. "Damn you, Bren," Ryse muttered.

Avery sighed and laughed. "It's okay, take him home. We can finish this later."

He kissed her once more before he left. As she drove, she realized for the first time in her life she was going to have a man in her bed.

"You bastard," Ryse said as Brenden laughed his ass off. "For the love of Zeus, why did you honk the horn?"

Brenden finally stopped laughing long enough to answer. "Oh come on Ryse, what were you going to do? Cop a feel right in the middle of the parking lot? You had that poor woman's dress hiked up to her waist. You know you can't have her like this. What happens when she finds out about *us?*"

Ryse scrubbed a hand over his face. Damn but Avery made him insane with need.

Brenden had a point. He needed to cool down, get his bearings back, and remember why they had come for Avery in the first place. She was about to have her entire world turned upside down and inside out. After it was all said and done, she might end up hating Ryse for being the one who screwed up her life.

"You're right. Call the team. Tell them to start packing. We've got to wrap this up before I do something stupid."

Before Brenden made the call, he reminded Ryse of one last fact. He was a Thracian soldier and Avery was a Divine Grace—whether she knew or not—and their attraction was a biological curse from the gods. If he acted on his urges before she had the knowledge of her destiny, they would punish him severely. And Avery might truly hate him for all his lies.

That sobered him up fast.

Ryse helped his men pack up their computers and bags. Tonight they left, period. Hammon had already erased their memory from the minds of the landlords. Brenden was the only tenant they would recall. He would complete his mission and exit quietly after they retrieved Avery.

Yankee, Cutter, and Philippe loaded bags into the SUVs. Judging by the scowl on Yankee's face, he had something on his mind. Ryse asked what was up.

"Look, boss, are you sure we got the right chick?"

"Yes," Ryse said with unequivocal conviction. "Why do you ask?"

"Well, I don't know, Hammon's been doing the monk meditation thing for three days now and can't get a read off her."

"That's not what I said," Hammon cut in, his African accent making each word a staccato beat. He carried a crate of surveillance equipment from the next room.

"You said you didn't sense power." Yankee argued.

Hammon's retort was calm and even. "I said that it was difficult to sense her power. Not that I couldn't."

Yankee rolled his eyes and shook his head. "Whatever. Same shit." A couple other men grinned at the exchange. There were never two personalities as opposite as Hammon and Yankee.

He turned to Ryse. "Don't you think we should make sure, I mean *damn* sure she's the one before we kidnap her?"

"Yankee, I know she's the one." Ryse handed him a laptop cord to load into the case.

"How? The chick is hot; I'll give you that. You have good taste if nothing else. She's a sweet piece of a—"

"Yankee!" Ryse said with a finger in his face. "Finish that sentence and I'll strangle you with the computer cord."

"Sorry." He held up his hands in surrender. "Just making a point."

Ryse looked around to make sure the other men weren't listening too carefully, then leaned in. "I *know,* Yankee. I know down to my very bones that she's the one."

"Are you sure you're not thinking with one of those bones?" Yankee whispered back.

Ryse chuckled and let out a sigh. "By Ares, you are a pain in the ass."

"Everyone has to excel at something, boss." Yankee grinned and popped the collar of his leather jacket.

"Just get this stuff packed up. I have to go charm my woman."

A loud crash brought both men to attention. They ran into the next room where Hammon stood motionless, his eyes glowing white. At his feet was a broken laptop. Cutter bent to pick up the pieces.

"This isn't a normal rogue," Hammon whispered, his voice shaking. He turned those white-glow eyes to Ryse. "We must go to her! NOW!"

CHAPTER SEVEN

AVERY PULLED OFF her boots and flopped down in her favorite chair. She'd started a fire in the sitting room. Firewood was cheaper than turning on the main heater. It was cozier too.

She tried not to get nervous about Ryse coming over as she checked her clock. It was about one in the morning. They would probably fall asleep as soon as they both relaxed. Avery watched the fire dance around the bricks of the firebox. It comforted her. Something about having a fire going in the house made her feel safe and strong.

The knock at the door woke her up. Two o'clock. She'd dozed off. She turned on the porch light and opened the door.

"What took so—" Avery stopped speaking when she realized the person at her door wasn't Ryse. She looked into a set of bloodshot green eyes. "*Jerry.* What are you doing here?"

There was something in his eyes Avery had never seen before. It wasn't alcohol induced and it gave her chills.

"You going to invite me in?" he asked coldly. The ice made Avery's heart pound. He was radiating anger and vengeance, very unlike the Jerry she knew.

Avery tried to keep her calm, but it was quickly turning into sheer panic. Something was wrong with her friend. "Of course darlin.'" She took his hand and led him in. "Your hands are freezin.' How long have you been out in the cold?"

"I was afraid I would wake you, but you're still in your dress.

Waiting on someone?"

"Jerry," she pleaded as she pushed him into the living room close to the fire. "Please tell me what's going on. You've been actin' strange for the last couple days."

"You'll never learn, will you?"

"What?"

Avery knew the next sound well. It was a sound that sent terror flying through her body, the sliding *click* of the safety being flipped off a gun. When she turned her head, she stared at the wrong end of a barrel.

"I told you not to let strangers in your house."

"W—what are you doing?" Her voice was no longer strong. He pressed the gun harder against her forehead.

"Finishing what was started ten years ago. Sit down." He pushed her into one of the dining room chairs.

Mentally, she went over every lesson in self-defense she ever had. If she could get to the closet by the door, she had a pistol. But Jerry was too close. She analyzed how he was standing. If she could just get the gun away from him.

With all the speed and muscle she had, Avery grabbed the chair she was sitting in and hurled it at Jerry. It knocked him out of the way, but he didn't lose the gun. He stumbled back, cursed, and let one round go. It hit the wall. Avery broke for her gun in the closet, but wasn't fast enough.

"You bitch!"

The butt of the gun hit her in the side of the head and everything went black.

Frank was pretty bummed. He'd had fun tonight, but it was for show. For Avery. Ryse made her happy and while he was glad, he was also heartbroken. He'd spent many years of his life looking after her, watching for the threat he knew was coming. It was a gut feeling. Avery was special, something out of this world special. But she didn't belong to him.

And what was up with Jerry? He picked up the phone to call his partner and make sure he'd arrived home safely. There was no answer. He cursed the cop in him that needed to make sure Jerry was safe and made a U-turn to head to his place.

Frank's stomach curdled when he saw the front door busted open. He pulled out his firearm and radioed the station about a possible break in.

Raising his gun and flashlight, he called out to Jerry twice before entering. Nothing on the inside of the house was out of place. He searched every room. No Jerry. Then he noticed the kitchen pantry was lit from within. When he opened the accordion doors, he saw a hidden staircase.

For two years this guy had been his partner. Countless times Frank had been over to his house, looked in this pantry, and never noticed the trap door that now stood haphazardly open. Someone had left in a rush.

Inhaling deep to calm his raging heartbeat, Frank slowly made his way down the staircase. At the bottom was a long, dark tunnel. It continued on for at least a hundred yards before arriving at another staircase. Frank took a ragged breath. Why would Jerry need a hidden tunnel into the abandoned house next door?

He took the stairs slowly, not wanting to alert anyone to his presence. At the top of the stairs a small piece of the wooden floor was pushed aside. Frank slowly rose from the hole. The room was empty, but what he found made his knees shake.

He examined the wall of photos and handwritten notes. Some items had once been in Avery's house. One picture of her had a knife driven into the wall right between her eyes. Every picture of himself had been disfigured.

"Sonofabitch!" Frank ran up the stairs, dialing his phone at the same time. "Pick up, Avery. Pick up!" he shouted into the ringing cell. When she didn't answer, he knew his worst fear had come to fruition. His best friend was in danger—again.

Minutes later he pulled into Avery's driveway. His phone rang. "Billings," he answered.

"Frank, it's Ryse."

"Jerry's some sort of stalker." Frank rambled about what he'd found. "I'm at her house now. I called in backup."

"Frank!" Ryse yelled. "This is far above anything you've ever dealt with. Do not engage. Understand? Do. Not. Engage!"

Frank hung up the phone. *Screw that!* Avery was in trouble and he was not about to let her get hurt.

Pain. That was all she felt. Pain that started in her head and went to her toes. Her eyelids fluttered open. She was in the sitting room by the fire, tied to a chair. She closed her eyes again to see if she could clear the dizziness. Rope kept her in the chair; her feet and hands were bound with duct tape.

"Good morning, sunshine," Jerry crooned as he grazed a hand down her cheek.

When she could open her eyes and not see triple, she focused on Jerry. He sat on the couch, gun in one hand and beer in the other. Stone faced and eyes like death, he glared at her.

"Why?" she coughed out, tears forming in her eyes.

"I've got to tell ya, baby girl, your lack of knowledge is almost insulting." He sloshed beer on her hardwood floors when he stood. "Of course, I really can't talk. If the idiots that tried to get to you the first time had understood Olympian culture better, I wouldn't have to be in this shithole town."

He pulled a book off her shelves and flipped through a few pages. It was one of her mother's books on Greek mythology and gods. "Where is it? Ah yes, here we go. It talks about you. Right here." He pointed to the paragraph and shoved the book in her face. "It says that you are to be pure when paired and bonded to your mate. Well, here's the kicker. You ready? See when my buddy came around a few years ago, you remember him, right? When he came to see you, he assumed that raping you would take care of that whole purity problem."

Jerry tilted his head and smiled. He spoke to her as he would a young child or a dog. His voice sounded sickeningly whimsical. "But you know what they say about assuming? Makes an ass out of you and me." He pointed a finger at her, then himself, and chuckled.

He acted drunk, but Avery feared she was seeing the real Jerry for the first time.

"Unfortunately, it wasn't until about four years ago that he realized taking your virginity still left you in the pure category. The book means *spiritual* purity, not physical. Damn loopholes!" Jerry laughed and it made Avery ill. "Just think, baby girl, all these years and that little incident was all for nothing. Pity, huh?"

"Why? Why me?" Avery cried.

"Because you're so special baby." He said it kindly, as if it were a real compliment. Jerry realized Avery was completely in the dark about all this. "You really don't know? That sucks!"

Avery spit out, "You're insane."

Jerry ran to her, gripped a hand full of hair and yanked her head backwards. "No, I'm *enlightened.*" He licked up the side of her neck, then released her hair with a violent push.

Avery's tears didn't stop her from being defiant. "You're a nutcase, Jerry. Frank will hunt you down—"

Jerry backhanded her hard enough to leave her cheek pulsating with pain. "You have no idea what is really out there in the world." Putrid anger lashed out of his mouth. He grabbed her face so hard it could've broken her jaw. "You think those men that raped you are monsters? Think I'm insane? Wait until you see who holds our leash, Avery. Just wait until he gets his hands on you. Then you will know what monsters really are."

Avery didn't let the hit intimidate her. She had nothing to lose. Glaring at him, his face not an inch from hers, she didn't look away.

"I'm not afraid of you." Her shaking voice denied the words of their power.

Jerry's lips flattened; his eyes went dead. He leaned down to whisper in her ear, "You should be. Do you know how many times I've nearly killed you? I've fantasized about stabbing you." He whipped out a knife and pointed it at her heart. "And I've nearly shot you a thousand times." With a shrug he put the knife away. "I've dreamt about strangling you." He trailed his fingers over her neck. "Every time I see your pretty skin I wonder how you taste, how your body would feel under mine—dead." He shuddered in pleasure then gained his composure again. "Frank's been such a help. He knows you better than anyone, so

I had to get close to him. What better way than to be his partner?" He laughed and flopped back down on the couch.

Pieces of his sick puzzle began to fall into place with a gut-wrenching click. Two years ago Frank's partner had been killed protecting a child during a gas station robbery. That's when Jerry came in to take his place.

"Officer Hernandez. That was you?" She openly wept for Officer Hernandez's family. "You bastard!" A burning sensation built in her chest.

Jerry held up his hands. "Guilty." His smile proclaimed he was proud of this. "He died a hero! What else did he want? Stupid cop."

"You sick fu—"

Jerry threw his beer bottle at the wall beside her head. "Enough of your mouth, bitch!" The glass shattered and beer splashed her. He shoved a rag into her mouth and taped it tight. The cloth made her gag. Panic rolled like waves in her soured stomach.

"He's here. You better play nice."

The front door of her house came crashing off the hinges, flying to the floor ten feet away. Avery's heart leapt out of her chest. She prayed Ryse or Frank came to her rescue.

That hope was quickly squashed when a hooded figure stepped inside.

It was the shadow of darkness, the devil incarnate. She couldn't see a face under the hood of his black cloak. But she could see the red flesh of his claw-like hands. Black talons stretched out like daggers. There was nothing human about him.

"I found thisss, lingering." The male voice was more animalistic than she expected. He waved his hands and a bloodied body flopped down on the floor.

Frank! Avery screamed into her gag.

CHAPTER EIGHT

FRANK WAS STILL alive, holding his throat like he had been strangled. He coughed and tried to crawl across the floor. "Avery," he coughed out, reaching for her.

Jerry grabbed him by the hair and pulled him up until he was on his knees. "Howdy, Frank! So glad you could join us."

"Quit playing with it." The cloaked figure hissed. "Thiss iss the one I care about."

"Leave her alone," Frank demanded in his weakened voice, his eyes never leaving Avery's face. His outburst earned him a brutal punch to the ribs.

A small army in red uniforms spread out over her house. Another man, bald, small, and fragile, shadowed the cloaked figure wearing monk's robes. His hand never disconnected from the cloak, he consistently touched his master.

With Frank here, things had changed. Avery didn't care if she died, but she didn't want him to suffer for her. He'd suffered for years because of her. Frank had borne her pain and loved her even when she couldn't love him back the way he wanted. He'd spent most of his life waiting and tending to her needs and he deserved better than to die like this.

"She's done nothing so far," Jerry spoke to the demon. "But she's one of them. Otherwise the Thracians wouldn't have come."

"I sssensse their Massster. Ssshe must be sspecial." He approached

Avery and she squirmed to get away. Evil clouded around him. He reeked of acid and her stomach revolted.

"Sssuch a wasste."

Lifting a talon to her cheek, he made a thin slice in her flesh. Then he leaned in to slick out a serpent's tongue across the bleeding cut. "Deliciousss."

His tongue burned her, like he'd poured alcohol over the open wound on her face.

"May I have her first?" Jerry asked. "I've been waiting for two years to screw her." He reached down and grabbed himself. "Doesn't matter if it's before or after she's dead. I do like it when they fight back though." He leered at Avery.

"I believe I would enjoy watching that."

Avery fought harder against her restraints. *Oh god!* No. This couldn't be happening. Not again.

Deep inside the core of her body something stirred. The white-hot acid spread to the rest of her body.

"Don't touch her you sonofabitch!" Frank strained against Jerry's hold. He outweighed his captor by a good thirty pounds, but Jerry was much stronger than he looked.

"Okay, enough of you, too!" Jerry pulled out his gun and pressed it to Frank's temple.

"NO!" Avery screamed into the gag. It came out as a muffled roar. Anger blazed inside her. Lava ran through her bone marrow and into every cell of her body.

"What's up with her eyes?" Jerry pointed at her with his gun.

"Ahh," mused the demon. "She'sss awakening." He took a step back, but not in fear. He was observing. "Hurting thisss human angersss her. Do it ssslowly."

Jerry put the gun down and pulled out a knife from his boots. His smile turned into something unholy as he plunged the knife into Frank's arm. Blood poured from his arm when the knife was pulled out. Frank tried to contain his reaction, but Avery could see the pain in his eyes.

She fought harder, something primal taking over her body. Tremors raked her limbs. Something was wrong with her. Fever spread over her skin and sweat dripped down her face.

Tilting his head and stepping back, the cloaked demon lifted his hand and Jerry plunged the knife into Frank's side. This time he cried out and Avery's heart hammered in her chest.

The world began to spin and shadows crossed her vision. She clamped her eyes shut. Every nerve ending in her body was on fire.

"Fire keeper. Incrrredible," said the demonic man. "Let'sss sssee what you can do." The army watched, guns pointed at her.

The smell of something burning pierced her consciousness. The ropes and duct tape binding her were smoking; her chair got hot. When she opened her eyes, the world had taken on a red tint. The gag fell out of her mouth and she roared like a beast.

"Again!"

Another patch of blood appeared on Frank's shirt from where Jerry struck him. This time, she knew it had pierced too close to his heart.

Frank gasped and tried to suck in a breath before falling to the floor. "Avery!"

He was dying in front of her and she could do nothing to stop it. A well of hatred sprang from within her.

For more than a decade Frank had been her friend, confidant, protector, family, and source of unconditional love. Memories of their years together flashed before her eyes. Bright happy smiles, loving embraces, kind words, tear provoking laughter, all the beauty that made up her best friend bubbled up inside of her. Watching him die would rip her soul apart.

With that, the dam broke and Avery let the inferno take over. Rage consumed her and filled her every cell. Raw power invigorated her body. When she pulled against the ropes this time, they gave way and fell to the floor. Avery looked down at her body. Flames licked up her skin, skimming gently over the surface, but not penetrating. Her clothing disintegrated, eaten by the fire. Every inch of her body glowed, but she wasn't burning.

In fact, Avery had never felt better.

"Kill her," the demon commanded.

Bullets tickled as they hit her, but melted upon contact. She brushed them off without any harm done. Narrowing her eyes at the demon, she ran and tackled him. He clawed and fought against her hold, but his talons went right through her incorporeal form. As the cloak began to burn, he cried out for the bald man. The instant they touched, they disappeared.

Her focus shifted to Jerry advancing on her. He shot two rounds that should have hit. It was no different than shooting into a wall of fire. She never felt them pass through her.

"You bastard!" She instinctually grabbed his throat. Frightened eyes bulged out of his head as a blowtorch of flames consumed him. The inferno pushed his body back on the couch. His screams were music to her ears. Justice. This was his punishment for Hernandez, for Frank, and every other innocent person he'd ever hurt. The onslaught of flames continued even after Jerry's screams subsided.

Those screams gave her satisfaction.

"Avery!" A deep voice penetrated her anger. It was the only voice she was *not* expecting.

She froze as Ryse rushed over to protect her. Turning to look at him, she noticed a battle being fought. Men in black leathers were fighting men in red uniforms. Ryse yielded a blade as long as her arm with the skill of a seasoned warrior.

He barked out orders to the men wearing the black leathers even as he separated a head from its body with one slice of his mighty sword. The two parts made a wet *thunk* against her floor when they fell.

One of the last remaining red soldiers pointed his gun at her and fired off three rounds. *Hasn't he learned yet?* When she focused her hate-filled gaze on him, his eyes widened in fear. Avery approached and he fell backwards over the logs by the fireplace. She picked him up by his clothes. Power and anger mixed inside her, making everything in her mind hazy and red. Everywhere she touched him smoldered.

"Who was he?" she demanded. "Who was that *thing* in the cloak?"

The soldier could only flail in pain, fighting to get her flaming hands off him. Before she even knew what he'd done, Ryse grabbed the soldier from Avery's hands. With one quick, well-practiced movement, Ryse snapped his neck and dropped him to the floor, nothing more than another log to be put on the fire.

Ryse's long leather jacket swished around his body. He had a sword in one hand and the other was held out to her, palm up.

"Avery, take my hand. It will make the fire stop." He spoke slow and soft.

"I don't want it to stop!" Avery bellowed. Amazing strength within her had finally been released. Her veins sizzled with the invigorating power running through them. "They killed Frank's partner, and now they've killed Frank. I want them to all to die." She didn't recognize her own voice.

One of the other men spoke in a language Avery didn't know. He had curly black hair that framed his face. Ryse responded in the same language, then looked at her. "Frank isn't dead, Avery. But you can't go to him until you calm down."

Avery spun around to locate Frank. He lay on the floor surrounded by blood. His chest barely moved. Bent over him was a tall, thin man with skin as black as night. He tried desperately to stop the bleeding, but there were too many wounds.

Ryse was right; burning as she was, she wouldn't be able to touch or hold him. The hardwood floor was already burning under her feet. Fear of what she had become took over her mind, clearing away the haze of anger. With sorrow and panic, she looked back to Ryse.

"How? How do I make it go away?"

"I will help you." The curly haired man had traded places with Ryse. He now stood a couple feet from her. "Give me your hand." His accent made his English choppy.

"I'll burn you."

"Not me, *Principessa.* Take my hand. Trust me."

Avery took his hand and he closed his eyes on contact. She expected him to scream from the pain, so the serene smile on his face was surprising. Springing from his touch was a chill that counteracted her flames. As the cold slowly spread from her hand to her arm and then into the rest of her body, the flames receded. Avery stood there, naked and shaking. Dizziness nearly took her under. She shook her head to clear it away. It didn't matter. All that mattered was Frank. She fell to his body, holding his face in her hands. The black man worked around her, meeting her eyes only once.

"Frank! Frank! Look at me! Frank!" she screamed through her tears. She shook his face until his eyes opened. "Can you hear me?"

"Avery." His hand found her arm and she held onto him. "Hey kiddo." The effort it took to speak made him cough up blood.

"Shh, shh. I'm right here."

Two large black hands worked to stop the bleeding. There was so much blood. The Italian joined him in attempting to freeze the injuries and stop blood loss. Their efforts were useless.

"I love you, Avery," Frank whispered as his eyes rolled back.

"No, no, no, Frank!" His eyes opened again. "Don't you do that! Damn it! Don't you say goodbye. I need you Frank, you can't leave me."

"Go with him, Avery." Frank left no doubt in Avery's mind who he was talking about. Ryse stood over them looking down. "Take care of her."

Ryse bent down and locked hands with Frank. "I will, my friend. With my life, I will."

Avery bent to kiss him. She pressed her lips to his already cooler skin. "I love you, Frank! I love you so much. Forgive me."

"Nothing to forgive kiddo. I love . . ."

She pulled her head back to see the silent peace of death on his face.

The wail that escaped her throat rippled though him in a wave of terror. Ryse bent to close Frank's eyes, and then pulled Avery into his arms. Her body shook as she sobbed and screamed in pain.

What a damned mess. Ryse couldn't believe he'd let Frank die.

"Boss, look, the police will be here soon." Bren stood in the entryway of the house wearing his police uniform, eyes locked on Avery and Frank. Ryse noticed the shadows taking over his eyes.

"Brenden!" Ryse yelled to get the sentinel's attention.

Blinking and focusing on his Master's face, he finished his thoughts. "Frank called in the break in at Jerry's, told them he was coming here. I called in the response so I can help clean things up. But you have got to get her the hell out of here."

"Master." Hammon said from beside him, his black eyes matched his skin and were full of calm determination and focus. "She must die to this life. It is the only way."

That got Avery's attention. "No!" she shrieked.

"We have to stage your death. It's the only way local authorities won't look for you." Ryse scooped her up in his arms, ignoring her protest. Philippe helped wrap her in a quilt. Ryse yelled out orders as he rushed to the back door of the house.

Ryse, Cutter, and Philippe ran as fast as they could to the woods behind Avery's house. They had parked the SUVs on the other side of the little patch of forest. Ryse only looked back to see Bren's police cruiser come to life with sirens and lights.

His men would take care of the story and the clean up. Right then his only concern was getting Avery the hell out of there and as far away from this place of death as possible.

None of this had gone as planned. Where had those rogues come from? How did they get to Avery's home so fast? The enemy had a teleporter. It was the only explanation. Gods! That would shift the balance of this war.

Ryse cradled Avery closer to his chest and heard her cry. Each sob broke his heart. What would she do now? Would she ever get over the carnage and horror of tonight?

He sent up prayer to the gods for peace and comfort to be bestowed on her. She was going to need all their divine help she could get to fulfill her destiny.

Continue on Avery's journey in

Divine Destiny

The Divine Chronicles

Excerpt from Divine Destiny, The Divine Chronicles Book 1

Divine Destiny

By JoAnna Grace

From Progressive Rising Phoenix Press

Chapter One

AVERY looked back see her home engulfed in flames. The orange and yellow stretched to the sky as if crying for help. Every memory, every texture, and smell of home would be gone in a matter of minutes. When the roof collapsed, Avery covered her mouth before the scream could escape. Instead, she buried her head in the neck of the man carrying her through the woods and away from the nightmare she had just experienced.

She sobbed silently and hit her fist against his chest. Though he'd promised to carry her to safety, she didn't know if she believed that. Only moments ago Avery had watched him kill mercilessly. It might have been to rescue her, but a normal person didn't kill with such precision and no remorse.

Then again, a normal person didn't burst into flames and incinerate her attackers.

Ryse's cell phone rang just before the car veered off the interstate to go south. "Ryse," he answered with clipped tone.

"Master," answered his second in command in his African accent. Hammon had been with him for centuries. "All evidence of our time here is gone. No one will remember us. Philippe held off the flames so we could gather some of her personal belongings before we escaped. Brenden will continue his ruse as an officer. Cutter will make sure all believe Avery and Frank were killed in a lover's quarrel with Jerry. All other bodies have been taken care of. Yankee was able to get the Lady's dogs out before anyone arrived."

"Good. Everyone will meet up at the safe house. Tell Brenden to stay behind, finish out his job, then get to the Haven. We don't know if they will come back and I don't want him there if they do."

"Yes, sire. We are not far behind you."

Ryse hung up his phone and cast a quick glance at his passenger in the back seat. She was a mess. He knew beneath the quilt was a bloodied, shaken body and more emotional scars than one woman should have to carry. Her beautiful face was bruised, her cheek was gashed, and tears had cut tracks in the soot that clung to her skin.

His mission had been to get her out safely and calmly. Instead, his presence had alerted the enemy in hiding. Ryse hadn't known how close they had been all along. By the time he found out, there had been no time to explain, no time to coax her trust or comprehension. There was only time to save her and get the hell out.

Jerry had known quickly what Ryse was. Olympians could shield their auras—hide them completely if needed. However, a powerful Olympian like Ryse could not be contained by such magic. Any Olympian within a five-mile radius could sense him even with his aura shielded to the best of his abilities. Jerry knew that if Ryse got too close, his chance to kill Avery would be lost. His success would have been hell for Ryse.

Thank the gods Ryse and his Elites had arrived in time to find Avery alive. What he hadn't expected was to find her on fire, the brilliant flames dancing along her skin and burning away her clothing. She had been ethereal, a red and orange glowing goddess, her long curls floating about her head and alive with the fire. He stood paralyzed by her deadly beauty before he fully comprehended what it meant. Helioan fire keepers were rare. It was a good thing Philippe had been there to counteract her heat with his cold.

Her soft voice broke into his thoughts. "Where are you taking me?" He nearly choked at the fear in her words.

"Somewhere you will be safe."

"Those people who tried to kill me, you didn't get them all. There was one that, well, he just *vanished.*" She sounded like she didn't believe her words. "How is that possible? How is any of this possible?"

"Their leader had a Teleporter. There aren't many left in our world, but they can transport themselves anywhere in the blink of an eye."

Her voice trembled. "In your world? What world is that?"

Ryse looked back at his charge. "The world of Olympians, Avery, the descendants of the gods. Your parents didn't live to bring you home, but now that I've found you, it's time for you to take your place among us."

"This can't be real. I'm in a horrible nightmare." Avery said, fresh tears dripping down her face. "My friends will search for me."

"I'm afraid not, love." He looked back quickly, then turned away again. "They will all believe you're dead."

He could hear her sobbing and mumbling, see her rocking herself in the back seat. "I'm going to be sick." She grabbed for the handle to open the door and Ryse swerved to stop the car on the side of the road just as she lost the contents of her stomach. Luckily the interstate wasn't busy this time of night and only a handful of cars passed them. Ryse came to her side, made sure her nakedness was covered and held back her hair.

"Avery, I can make you sleep if you wish." He prayed she took the offer.

"You're going to drug me?" She began to scramble out of his hold.

"No. No, I swear. I can simply put your mind to sleep so that you have relief from this agony. Please let me help you. Your body needs to rest." He tilted her chin up until her eyes met his. He'd fallen for those green eyes the moment they first connected with his two days ago. "Please. I won't hurt you."

For a long moment she stared at him unblinking. He wondered if her shattered mind even recognized what he'd said. Instead, she dropped her eyes and turned her face away. "Just make it all go away."

Ryse picked her up and laid her down across the back seat, tucking the quilt around her. He placed his hand over her forehead and closed his eyes, praying to the gods. As he spoke the sacred prayers, his hand began to glow with a soft white light and Avery's eyelids slid down. The power of his aura flooded her body. He thanked the gods and watched for a moment as Avery relaxed into a deep sleep. She would need her strength in the days to come. Avery's life would never be the same.

MEET THE AUTHOR:

JoAnna Grace lives in a world of alpha males and strong females where true love conquers all—at least in her mind!

From the time she started holding a crayon she began to create magical worlds. Her first book was a series of pictures about a puppy princess. The story changed each time she told it, but there was always a happy ending! Her first written story was about girls who changed into tigers.

Now those stories have become a bit more complex.

JoAnna's tales are spun at her home in East Texas where she lives with her husband, three kids, and a couple dogs. When not hiding behind the computer screen you can find her camping, boating, and shopping.

Sign up for her newsletter to receive information about new releases, events, and giveaways!

www.authorjoannagrace.com

JoAnna loves to hear from readers and fans!
You can find her at the following places:

Authorjoannagrace.com
Twitter: @JoAnnaGrace4ya
Facebook: Jo Anna Grace Author

Available now from JoAnna Grace and Progressive Rising Phoenix Press

Divine Destiny

The Divine Chronicles Book 2

The gods work in mysterious ways . . .

Avery McClain is normal. Or so she thinks.Until her life is shattered and she is rescued by a Thracian warrior. He takes her to the Haven, a realm of safety for the magical race of Olympians. There she discovers her life was meant for a higher calling as the mate of an Olympian Prince. Her choice will change everything.

Ryse Castille has one job: convince Avery to step into her role as a Divine Grace. As with any mission, there are obstacles to overcome. Including the fact he is captivated by her. Of all the gifts the gods have given him, romance was not included. But Avery belongs to him and he will stop at nothing to protect her. The enemy might be closer than they think.

Available in Print and Ebook

Available now from JoAnna Grace

Divine Judgment
The Divine Chronicles

One warrior fights for the love of his life, while another warrior finds his.

The gods have summoned . . .

Thracian Master, Ryse Castille, and Deities around the world travel to the Heavens and face their creators. It's time for a murderer to come to justice and Ryse will have a front row seat at the trial. The Heavens have a few unexpected surprises for him; he prays one of them will be a reunion with his beloved Avery's spirit. He'll stop at nothing to bring her home safely and see his father's killer brought to justice—if the gods don't destroy the Olympian race first. Their fate rests on his shoulders.

While the Master is away . . .

Elite Apprentice, Dante, has a monumental responsibility in Ryse's absence. He must watch over the widowed queen and Avery's comatose body until her spirit is returned. In the wake of the king's death, the gods send Lysandra, an Oracle, to earth to guide them through the troubling times. Weighed down by the constant disapproval of his father, Dante finds solace in her admiring eyes. Their unexpected affections are cultivated amidst the secrecy and constant threat of exposure. Both Oracle and Elite are bound by their oaths—the very things that might wrench them apart.

Two Warriors.

Two Quests.

One Final Judgment.

Available in Print and Ebook

Available Now from JoAnna Grace and Dark Red Press:

Pride Before the Fall

The Blake Pride Series

Feline shape shifter Vivian Blake is every bit the alpha female- on stage and on four legs. She commands the audience with her husky voice and sexy dance moves as confidently as she leads her family. The four other members of her Pride depend on her to keep them safe. They are on the run from a sadistic Pride alpha named Trace who wants revenge after nearly dying under Vivian's claws. To protect her family, Vivian does what ever it takes, including private dances.

Kasey Blackburn is alpha of the most powerful wolf and bear mixed Pack in the country. And he's not too happy about a group of renegade felines moving in and turning tricks in his city. But one look at Vivian and his intentions change. Too bad she's a feline under a death sentence. As well, certain members of his Pack aren't too keen on Vivian's nighttime activities. They don't want to see their alpha mate with a stripper. When Vivian comes into heat, the tigress within wars with the human side. The cat wants a mate but the woman wants escape. Can Vivian resist the promise of a fresh start with Kasey or will her pride cost her everything?

Available in Print and Ebook

Available from JoAnna Grace

Break Her Fall

The Blake Pride Series

As beta female of the Blake Pride, Amilynn does whatever it takes to get the job done and guard her family—even if it might not be morally sound. Now that the Pride has moved in with the Blackburn Pack, she faces a threat she never saw coming . . . a *mate.* The sexy and persistent wolf wants to claim the leopardess, but she's not going down without a fight.

Ezekiel is used to getting what he wants and his eyes are set on his seductive target. Yet predicting Amilynn's next move is fruitless. He's caught between admiring her strength and resenting it. Does he dominate or submit? Can he prove to Amilynn she really is worth the fight?

When a ghost from Amilynn's past stalks their family, Ezekiel will learn her true strength. Amilynn isn't a docile house cat and, by the time she's done, everyone will know it.

Available in Print and Ebook.

Available Now from JoAnna Grace

The Roles We Play

She's a woman who values her privacy. He's a man always in the spotlight. Can they make it work after he brings her painful past into the public eye?

Kelly prefers to *take* the pictures, not to be in them. With her grandfather, she lives a solitary life in an isolated estate home. When her best friend wakes her up in the middle of the night asking for a favor, Kelly never dreamed it would land her face-to-face with her celebrity crush.

Trevor lives his life in front of the cameras. He's one of the top super stars of Hollywood—and he's on the brink of a burn out. Before he takes on another film, he escapes to a secluded place to get his mind straight. He didn't expect to have his entire way of thinking turned upside down by his lovely, yet blunt hostess. As the walls between them come down, Trevor allows Kelly to review his next project, a movie that hailed the negative side of BDSM. The subject hits far too close to home and her confession changes his perspective. Now that Trevor has seen things through Kelly's eyes, it sets him on a new path, one he can't reveal until the time is right. But she harbors a secret of her own.

Can their love survive the truth? Or will their new roles tear them apart?

Available in Print and Ebook

49259340R00048

Made in the USA
Charleston, SC
18 November 2015